This **Picture Mammoth** *belongs to*

_____

_____

First published in Great Britain 1996
by William Heinemann Ltd
Published 1997 by Mammoth
an imprint of Egmont Children's Books Ltd
239 Kensington High St, London W8 6SA

10 9 8 7 6 5 4 3

Text copyright © Susan Hampshire 1996
Illustrations copyright © Maria Teresa Meloni 1996
Susan Hampshire and Maria Teresa Meloni have
asserted their moral rights

0 7497 3023 4

A CIP catalogue record for this title is available from the British Library

Printed in Hong Kong by Wing King Tong Co. Ltd

Rosie's
First Ballet Lesson

Susan Hampshire

illustrated by Maria Teresa Meloni

For her first ballet lesson Rosie's mother bought her
a pair of pale pink ballet shoes.
They were the prettiest shoes Rosie had ever seen.

Soon the day came for Rosie's first lesson. The ballet teacher was called Madame.
"Hello Rosie," she said. "Please put on your ballet shoes, and then come and meet the other children."

After she put on her new ballet shoes, Rosie said hello to the
the rest of the class. Their names were Tommy, Sally, Jasmine,
Yuko, Rani, Chuck and Rudolph.

"And this is Miss Melody, who plays the piano,"
said Madame. Miss Melody smiled and her fingers ran up
and down the piano keys like mice.

It was time for the ballet lesson to begin.
"Now children," said Madame, "sit on the floor, with
your legs straight out in front, and point your toes like
sharp pencils."
Rosie sat in a row with the other children and Madame
showed them how to point their feet in time to the music.

"Now, what do we do after toes?" Madame asked.
"HANDS!" Rudolph shouted.
"That's right," said Madame. "I want you to shake your hands as though they're dripping with water."
Rosie shook her hands enthusiastically and made them as soft as rabbits' ears.
"See how pretty they look?" asked Madame. "These are our ballet hands."

Then Madame went to her bag and took out a little package. "Who knows their left foot from their right foot?" asked Madame. No one answered. Madame gave each child a red sticker and blue sticker. "These are to stick on to your ballet shoes so that you'll know which is your left foot and which is your right foot. Watch me and put the red sticker on your right heel and the blue sticker on your left heel."

Rosie carefully stuck the red sticker on her right shoe and the blue sticker on her left shoe.
"Now you know which part of your foot to show when you point - the inside of your foot and heel," said Madame.

Next Madame showed the children how to do points.
"Girls, please hold out your skirts like butterflies. Boys, hands on hips, backs as straight as ironing boards. Now we'll do three points with the right *red* foot, then we'll change feet, and do three points with the left *blue* foot."
Rosie looked down at the foot she was pointing. She could see a blue sticker so she knew that she hadn't made a mistake.

Next they practised skipping.
"Knees high, skirts held out, backs straight," Madame called as they skipped round the room.
Jasmine and Rani skipped so fast that they bumped into each other and fell in a heap on the floor. Madame shook her head at them.

"That was very silly," she said. "You must try to do every step properly. Think about your feet and really point your toes as you skip."

When Rosie had finished skipping, she was out of breath. She was glad that it was time to stand still and do knee bends. "Are these *pliés*?" Tommy and Sally asked Madame together.

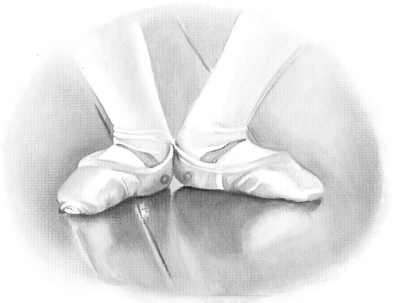

"Yes," said Madame. "These are *pliés* in first position, when your heels are together."

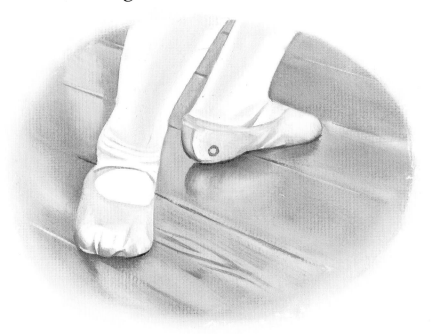

"But when your feet are apart and your toes are turned out, they are *pliés* in second position."

Then Madame showed the
children how to bend their
legs with their knees going
over their toes.

"I can do first position!" Rosie called to her mother, putting her heels together and pulling her knees straight. "And I can do second position too."

"Jasmine, please show me three positions of the arms. Remember to start by shaking your hands to make ballet hands," called Madame.
Jasmine started by putting her arms down below her tummy.

Then Jasmine put her arms in front as though she was holding a basket.
"This is first position," she said.
"Very good," said Madame.

Then Jasmine put her arms out to
the side like a scarecrow.
"This is second position," she said

And finally she
lifted them above her
head like a frame round
her face. "Fifth position! I like
fifth position best because I feel like
a real ballerina," Jasmine said happily.
"Very nice, Jasmine," said Madame.

"Now, who wants to jump and see if they can touch my hand with their head?" Madame asked.
"Oh! Jumps! Lovely," the twins cried.

"Remember, all the dancing steps have French names," said Madame. "A jump is called a *sauté*. So let's do a *sauté* with pointed toes and straight knees and see how high we can go." Rosie immediately started jumping up and down.
"What should we do each time we land?"asked Madame.
"Bend our knees in a *plié*," the class shouted back.

When the children had finished jumping, Miss Melody
played some beautiful music on the piano.
"Listen to the piano," said Madame. "First we're going to
dance like butterflies and then, when the music changes,
we're going to dance like animals."
Miss Melody played some quiet, pretty music and Rosie ran
lightly round the room fluttering her arms. Suddenly, Miss
Melody started playing some loud thumping music. Chuck
and Rudolph pretended to climb trees and ran after the girls
and tried to eat them.

Madame clapped her hands. "What do ballet dancers do when they have finished dancing?" she asked.

"Bow or curtsey!" the children cried together.

"Yes, this is our *revérence*," answered Madame. "Girls, hold out your skirts, then put your right foot behind your left foot and bend your knees. Boys, put your hand across your waist, bend forward from the hips and bow."

Rosie curtsied with the other girls, and the boys bowed.

"Thank you everyone," Madame said. "That's the end of our lesson for today. Make sure you practise at home and I'll see you all next week."

"Did you like your ballet lesson, darling?" asked Rosie's mother, giving her the ballet shoes to carry. Rosie nodded and smiled. She swung the shoes by their elastic, wanting everyone to see them.

But when they got back home, Rosie found that she'd lost one of her shoes.

"Oh Rosie, how could you be so careless!" said her mother. "We'll have to go all the way back."

Just then, there was a scratching at the door. It was Buster, Rosie's dog, with the missing ballet shoe in his mouth.

"Clever dog!" Rosie exclaimed, patting him happily.

After tea, Rosie put on her ballet shoes, and practised the steps she had learned.

"Toes like pencils, back straight as an ironing board," she said as she held out her skirt. "I love dancing. I want to dance and dance all day."

And then she skipped round and round the room pointing her toes while Buster sat and watched her, nodding his head from side to side in time to the music.